CH

To the friends who have helped me through dark times.

Boy Seeking Band is published by Stone Arch Books
1710 Roe Crest Drive, North Mankato, Minnesota 56003
www.mycapstone.com

Cataloging-in-Publication Data is available on the Library of Congress website.
ISBN: 978-1-4965-4448-3 (library hardcover)
ISBN: 978-1-4965-4452-0 (eBook)

Summary: Eighth-grade bass player Terence Kato is forced to transfer from a private arts school to a public school. He sets out to build a rock band and, in the process, make a few friends. He quickly locates a singer and keyboardist, but Terence wants to keep the rhythm going by finding a GUITARIST.

Cover illustration and design by Brann Garvey

Printed in the United States of America.
010368F17

GUITARIST WANTED

BY STEVE BREZENOFF

STONE ARCH BOOKS
a capstone imprint

TABLE OF CONTENTS

Terence Kato is a prodigy bass player, but he's determined to finish middle school on a high note. Life has other plans. In the middle of eighth grade, he's forced to transfer from a private arts school to a public school, where the kids seemingly speak a different language. But he knows a universal one: music. He sets out to build the city's greatest band.

Terence quickly locates his singer and keyboardist, but he wants to keep the rhythm going by finding a GUITARIST.

CHAPTER ONE

It's Sunday night, and Terence Kato couldn't be happier with the band so far.

His piano player, Claude, is on fire tonight.

Meredith "Eddie" Carson's vocals are as rich as a devil's food cake covered in honey.

Terence rethinks his metaphor, but his band is sounding great even in the crummy acoustics of Claude's basement practice room, which is nowhere near as impressive or state-of-the-art as that of potential bandmate Melody Ulrich.

Still, he's a lot more pleasant to be around than Melody, once again reminding Terence that his ability to judge people based on appearance is woefully inadequate.

Plus there was that whole probably-saving-Terence's-life from a couple bullies thing.

Bullying was never a problem back at Hart. But at a public middle school with a huge student population, it's bound to come up. And for Terence Kato, it has.

But that was last week. Ever since Claude stepped in just in the nick of time, the two colossal brutes haven't even looked sideways at Terence.

Claude ends their rendition of "Firework" with a piano flourish. It's not Terence's favorite song, but it was on his band's playlist at Hart. Polly Winger — his band's singer back then — always rocked it, and it was always a big crowd pleaser.

Eddie rocks it too.

"Great job, guys," Terence says.

"Thanks, boss," Eddie says with a wink at Claude. Claude snickers and covers the laughter with a fast arpeggio.

"Laugh if you want," Terence says as he unplugs his bass. "But someone needs to take the wheel."

"Says who?" Eddie says, sneering at him.

"Says me," Terence says. He lays his bass carefully in its case. "And I'm the only one of us who's been in a band before, right?"

Eddie shrugs. "I guess."

"So get us a gig," Claude says, getting back to his arpeggios.

"We're not ready for gigs," Terence says, almost laughing. "For one thing, we still need a guitar player and a dru —"

"What?" Claude says, finishing a scale with a dramatic A-minor chord. "We don't need a guitar player. I can handle everything right here on the ivories."

Terence shakes his head as he winds his cord and lays it on top of his bass case. "The set list has too much old soul, R&B, and rock to have no guitar. Beside, I love a guitar in a jazz combo too. Joe Pass? Wes Montgomery?"

Claude stares at him blankly. He glances at Eddie.

She cocks her head. "I have *Take Love Easy* on vinyl."

That's the first duet album with Joe Pass and Ella Fitzgerald, possibly the best vocalist of all time, in jazz or otherwise.

Terence flashes an impressed face and gets to his feet, his gig bag over his shoulder. "The point is, we need a guitar player."

"Well," Claude says, leaning back and cracking his knuckles, "lots of people play guitar."

"I play guitar," Eddie says.

"But most aren't very good," Claude says, looking at Eddie with a crooked wicked grin.

"Point taken," Eddie admits.

"Well," Terence says, "I'll ask around again. Though that didn't end very well when I tried to find a pianist."

"So leave it to us," Claude says as he rises from the piano bench to see the other bandmates out.

"Yeah," Eddie says. "We know all these kids already. And we wouldn't want you to put yourself in danger of making a *friend*."

Claude laughs, and Terence feels his face go hot. *Rule number one,* he thinks.

It's just easier without friends — especially when you consider why he left Hart Arts to begin with: dead mother, no money, and a dad who has completely checked out.

"That's fine with me," Terence says, and though his bass is heavy, he feels a weight lift from his shoulder. "The fewer people I have to talk to, the better."

"I heard you're looking for a guitar player," says a whispery voice at Terence's ear in advisory first thing Monday morning.

"Um," Terence says, keeping his eyes on the open book on his desk. It's a kind of how-to book on the bassists who played with funk, R&B, and soul great James Brown over the years, some of the best players in music history. "Where'd you hear that?"

He glances quickly to his right. It's a girl he knows — kind of. After all, he's been sitting next to her in advisory for two weeks now. *Sophia? Ophelia, maybe?*

"I overheard your friend Eddie asking a couple of seventh graders if they knew any guitarists," the girl whispers. "And she said she wants a girl."

Terence looks up. "A girl?" he says. "Why?"

"So she's not outnumbered?" the girl replies, shrugging. "I assume."

"Huh." Terence looks back at his book.

After a moment of silence, the girl asks, "So are you? Looking?"

Terence nods.

The girl scoots her chair a little closer. "You like James Brown?"

"Doesn't everyone?"

"I don't think most kids at this school know who James Brown is, Terry," the girl says.

So she knows his name. Sort of.

"I actually prefer Terence," he says, closing his book. "You'd have to audition."

She nods eagerly and smiles. "Of course."

"Can you stay after school a few minutes?"

She shakes her head. "I have lessons this afternoon."

She takes guitar lessons, Terence thinks. *I guess at least she's serious.* "Tomorrow?"

She shakes her head again. "After my lessons today," she says. "Like five?"

Terence thinks about the bike ride in the cold, assuming his dad is no help again.

He sighs. "Sure, I can do that. Where do you live?"

The girl tears the corner off a sheet of paper from her notebook and scribbles down her address.

Terence takes the paper and reads her name at the top. "Novia."

"That's me," she says. A moment later the bell rings to end advisory. "See you at five."

CHAPTER TWO

"I'm home!" Terence says as he walks into
the little rental home in Minneapolis and drops
his book bag next to the door.

Scratch that — rental *house*. This would never
be Terence's real home, and he'd vowed not
to let himself get too comfortable here, just as
he'd vowed not to let himself make new friends
at Franklin Middle School. Bandmates? Sure.
Friends? Never.

Terence almost expects silence in response.
He's gotten so used to Dad not being around,

or being asleep or half asleep in front of the TV when he is around. Would he be marathoning *Star Trek: The Next Generation* or *Battlestar Galactica* was the only real question.

So when Dad walks out of the little kitchen at the back of the house dressed in khakis and a collared shirt, Terence is stunned.

"How was your day?" Dad says as if it's the most normal thing in the world to say.

Which it is, of course — but not for this particular dad lately.

"Um, fine, I guess," Terence says, leaning on the back of the living room couch. It's the couch from their old house near Hart Arts: the color of milk chocolate, soft and leather, so no matter how many times and how often Terence has tried, he can't find the scent of Mom's perfume anymore. The smell of the leather is too strong. "Can you drive me to a friend's in an hour or so?"

Dad grins and puts an arm around Terence's

shoulders. "I'm so pleased you're making friends at your new school," he says.

Terence shrugs and pulls away a little. "So can you?"

"Sure," Dad says. He drops into his chair by the front window. It's also from the old house, as luxurious as the couch. Dad reclines and pulls out his phone.

"Um, Dad?" Terence says as he sits on the edge of the couch.

His father looks up from his phone and smiles. Terence hasn't seen that smile in months. Maybe that's why it looks so funny.

"What's going on with you, Dad?" Terence can't help but ask him.

Dad's smile freezes, not that it was moving and animated before. It just suddenly seems to be made of ice or something. Just as quickly, it shatters, and there's Dad's familiar flat frown. "I'm sorry," is all he says as he sits forward in his chair.

Terence leans back, and his head sinks into the leather couch cushions. The couch seems to exhale its strong, musky scent as the pillows give way to his weight.

"I've been depressed," Dad says. "Obviously. I'm — I'm having a hard time. And I haven't been much of a parent."

Terence sits up quickly. "I don't mean that," he says, and he wants to go on, but Dad cuts him off.

"It's fine. You're right." Dad puts his face in his hands, and soon he's silently sobbing, his shoulders bucking and the occasional croak escaping between his hands.

It's been a while since Dad cried in front of him — a few months at least. Terence is beside him and sitting on the arm of the recliner in moments, one arm around his dad. The first few times this happened after Mom died, it took him completely by surprise, and Terence sobbed right along with him.

Now, though, Terence has pretty much numbed to the outbursts, almost as if his job is to make sure Dad gets it out of his system quickly and remembers Terence is still there with him.

It works, and after less than a minute, Dad stops croaking and pulls his face out of his hands.

He takes a deep breath, staring into his still-open palms. "Sorry."

"It's OK," Terence says quietly.

Dad falls back in the recliner — his face flat, his eyes rimmed in red — and Terence hurries to his room. Hopefully when it's time to go to Novia's house, Dad will be back to wearing that frozen smile; riding with Dad — when he's sobbing or exhausted from sobbing — always reminds Terence of Mom's funeral back in July.

It was a hot day, and Terence sat sweating in a big black car in his too-big black suit with a black tie squeezing his neck too tight beside his father.

They held hands over the chasm of seat between them, and Dad held his handkerchief in his other hand. His eyes were already red and heavy and tired from crying when he said, "What are we gonna do, Ter-bear?"

Terence's little-kid pet name. Mom and Dad stopped using it years before.

But Terence didn't answer. He looked out the car window at the city on that Sunday — a regular day for everyone else.

It's five after five when Terence climbs out of the front seat of Dad's car. "You sure you don't mind waiting?" he says, leaning in the open door.

"Nah," Dad says. He holds up his phone. "I've got shows to catch up on."

"I won't be more than ten minutes or so," Terence says.

"I'll leave it running," Dad says, patting the dashboard near the heater knobs.

"You can probably come inside," Terence says. "If you want."

Dad seems to think about it for a moment, but he shakes his head. "Not much in the mood to meet parents and make small talk."

Terence understands that, and he closes the door and hurries down the path and onto the front porch. The inner door opens right away, but it's not Novia. It's a middle-aged woman with short brown hair and thick glasses with cat's-eye frames.

"Oh, excuse me," she says.

"Is Novia home?" Terence asks, stopping in front of her.

"Um, yes," she says, stepping around Terence. "We just finished her lesson. Excuse me." With that, she leaves the porch, climbs into the little hatchback parked at the curb in front of Dad, and drives away.

Novia appears in the doorway a moment later. "Oh, there you are," she says. "Come on in."

"I thought that was your mom," Terence says.

Novia laughs. "That's Priscilla, my music teacher."

Terence is surprised to hear that woman is a guitar player, but he doesn't say so. He just follows Novia inside. "Mom, my friend's here to hear me play guitar!"

Her mom calls back from somewhere deep inside the house, "OK! Keep the door open! Good luck!"

Novia looks at Terence and rolls her eyes. "Come on," she says, heading up the narrow stairs.

Terence follows her up and into her bedroom. It's narrow as well, with only a long desk on one side and a twin bed on the other. A small window between lets in some light until Novia flicks on the lamp, and the window becomes more like a little mirror at the end of the room.

Terence catches his own reflection in the window as he sits in the chair at the desk, and Novia drops to one knee to open her guitar case.

"So," Terence says, watching her pull out the acoustic guitar and check the tuning, "what do you like to play?"

"My mom taught me a bunch of folky nineties songs," Novia says as she sits on the edge of the bed and plays a big open G chord. She adds a seventh and plays it again. She adds a ninth and plays it again.

"Do you know any jazz?" Terence asks. So far, Novia doesn't seem promising to join the band. "Can you improvise at all?"

She twists up her mouth. "Not really," she admits. "I've only been playing for six months."

Six months? Terence thinks. *Why is she wasting my time?*

"I'm naturally pretty musical, though," she says as she strums the chord changes to what might be an Indigo Girls song. "I'm sure I'll pick it up quickly."

"Mmhm," Terence says.

Novia shifts on the edge of the bed, fixes her hair, and then starts a song in earnest: "Stubborn Love" by the Lumineers. Terence isn't a big fan.

Novia's voice is pleasant enough, but the guitar part is simple and folky, not at all the sort of music Terence wants for his band.

She plays through the first chorus and then stops. "What do you think?" she says, looking at Terence.

"Very good," he says. "You have a nice voice. But I don't know if your guitar playing is right for what we're doing."

"Oh," Novia says, obviously disappointed.

Terence stands. "Yeah," he says, pushing his hand through his hair and wondering how soon he can leave. "I mean, you obviously like folk music and stuff, but we're really — that is, we're looking for a real *virtuoso*, you know?"

Novia shrugs as she lays her guitar in its case.

"But stick with the lessons for sure," Terence says, moving toward the door. "You're doing great for only having played six months."

Novia closes the case as Terence starts to back down the stairs. "I don't take guitar lessons," she says.

"Oh, but . . . ," Terence starts. "I thought —"

Novia stops in the doorway and looks down the stairs at Terence. "You can let yourself out," she says and closes the door to her bedroom.

"How'd it go?" Dad asks when Terence gets into the front seat of the warm car.

"Fine," Terence says. "She's not good enough for the band though."

"Oh, too bad," Dad says, putting the car in drive. "I hope you let her down easy."

"I tried to," Terence says.

Dad pulls away from the curb, and Terence texts Eddie: *Any luck finding a guitarist?*

A moment later her reply comes: *Claude found someone to play this weekend.*

Then, a few seconds later she texts again: *He's REALLY good.*

CHAPTER THREE

He is really good.

It's Saturday morning, and the band is in Claude's basement again. Terence wishes now — more than ever — that he was standing in Melody Ulrich's cavernous basement. It had been set up like a recording studio, with a soundproof booth at the far end behind glass. Inside were mic stands, music stands, and a gleaming black grand piano.

Right now, they didn't need any of that stuff though. But they did need one thing: space.

That's because the band finally have their fourth. And no, Terence thinks, he doesn't actually wish he was at Melody's.

Like Eddie said, she wouldn't fit in with this bunch. But Desmond does.

Desmond has long hair and wears a black hoodie with a sleek black guitar slung around his neck and shoulders.

His changes are quick and tight. He plays along with Terence's jazzy bass line with no problem, following the tough changes. He's as good at guitar as Claude is at piano and Terence is at bass.

Eddie sits to the side, nodding along with the music and sometimes smiling.

So far, so good.

"Let's trade fours awhile," Terence says over the music.

Claude leaps into a wild, modal solo, banging away at the pkeys like only a jazz pianist can. When he's done, Terence picks it up and runs the neck, following Claude's modal lead but keeping it smooth instead of the choppy Thelonious Monk style Claude prefers on the keys.

He looks over at Desmond and nods as he reaches the end of his fourth measure.

Desmond flicks the knob on his guitar, sending the volume into the stratosphere, and then blasts off like a rocket into a mind-numbing and ear-piercing heavy-metal guitar solo.

Terence looks over at Claude on the piano as Desmond's fingers tap nearly every fret on his board, sounding more like Yngwie Malmsteen than Joe Pass. Claude shrugs back at him. Eddie's eyes go wide, and she leans back as if the blast of the guitar solo is a gust of wind.

As he plays his four-bar solo, he bangs his head up and down, sending his hair in a circular whip. His fingers are lightning across the fretboard. He's skilled, fast, talented — but it's not right for the song at all.

When he's done, Terence puts up a hand and closes his fist to the end the jam.

A moment later, they hear Claude's mother call down the basement steps. "Everything OK down there?"

"Yeah, Mom!" Claude shouts back. "Why do you ask?"

"It sounded like World War Three broke out!" she shouts back.

Desmond laughs. "That was nothing, right, guys?"

"Um, right," Claude replies. He calls up to his mom, "Sorry! We're just finishing up. We'll keep it down a bit."

"That's a relief," his mom replies. The basement door closes.

Terence unplugs his bass. "Thanks for playing with us, Desmond," he says. "That solo was something."

"Yeah!" Eddie says, jumping up from her seat. "That rocked."

"Thanks, guys," Desmond says as he packs up his guitar.

Claude rises from the piano bench and stands over Desmond, who kneels in the center of the room, zipping up his case. "Well, we'll let you know," Claude says, his voice deep and menacing.

Desmond stands as he backs away. "Um, OK," he says, his voice trembling a bit. "Thanks letting me jam."

With that, he hurries up the steps. They hear the muffled sounds of Claude's mom saying goodbye and the front door closing.

"You didn't have to scare him like that," Eddie says.

Claude shrugs. "Rejection is tough," he says. "Might as well make myself as scary as possible so he doesn't remember the part about having his feelings hurt."

"That," Terence says, "actually makes a little sense. It's twisted and bizarre, but it makes sense."

Claude laughs as he sits at the piano again. "Let's get that metal garbage out of our system."

"It wasn't *that* bad, you guys," Eddie says quietly, almost to herself.

"It was," Claude insists. He plays a quick chromatic run up the piano keyboard, and in moments Terence joins in. Before long, they're jamming on Terence's chord changes. Eddie even joins in with improvised lyrics and scatting.

It's fun. And they sound *good*.

Eddie is grinning and having a blast. Claude looks over at Terence, his eyebrows high and his smile wide.

Soon Claude's mom comes down the stairs, and they stop midjam.

"Sorry, Mom," Claude says. "We'll stop now."

"What?" she says, smiling. "I came down to watch and listen. You three sound fantastic!"

"We do, don't we?" Terence says.

"See?" Claude says. "We don't need a guitarist. We're a trio. It works."

"Especially that guitarist," Claude's mom says as she goes back up the stairs. "He kind of scared me."

Terence thinks a moment. They do sound good as a trio. Sure, a few of the songs in the set list need a guitar, but maybe the set list could stand some editing anyway.

"OK," Terence says, "then it's settled. We're a trio."

Eddie grins.

Claude plays a celebratory arpeggio. "Let's celebrate," he says.

"Paulie's!" Eddie says. She grabs her bag from the old couch behind the piano.

"My treat!" Claude's mom calls down the steps.

"Mom!" Claude shouts. "You were eavesdropping!"

"What?" she replies, sticking her head through the doorway at the top of the steps. "I'm excited!

CHAPTER FOUR

The three bandmates and Claude's mom slide into their favorite booth at Paulie's.

"Order anything you like," says Claude's mom as she quickly rises again from the booth. "I have to visit the little girl's room." She winks and hurries away.

"I need pineapple," Eddie says.

"On pizza?" Claude says, looking up from his menu. "That's literally a sin."

"They do it in Hawaii," Eddie says.

"Actually, I don't think that's true," Terence retorts. "I think they put SPAM on their pizza in Hawaii."

"What?" Eddie says, practically sneering at him. "That's ridiculous."

A moment later, their server steps up to the table. It's James, the sixteen-year-old server they had last time they were in, when Terence first met Claude.

"Oh, it's you three again," he says, filling their water glasses with his pitcher. "Where's your Neanderthal big brother?" he adds, sneering at Eddie.

"Oh, hi, James," Eddie says, her voice making it very clear that she's choosing the high road this time. "Are you having a nice Saturday?"

"Yeah, it's great," he says sarcastically. "I love taking orders from children and carrying hot pizza trays all day." He finishes pouring waters and then pulls a notepad and a pencil from his apron, which is stained with some crustified marinara sauce. "What do you want?"

"We haven't decided yet," Eddie says, flashing a big and phony grin. "Why don't you come back in two minutes to check again?"

James grins back and then rolls his eyes as he puts his pencil behind his ear and begins to walk off.

"Oh, James!" Eddie calls after him. "Why don't you make that three minutes."

He rolls his eyes and heads into the kitchen.

"He's a pleasure," Terence says.

"He always is, isn't he?" Eddie says, shaking her head.

As Claude's mom returns to the booth and slides in next to her son, the front door swings open, letting in the winter sunshine along with a family of five — including Novia, the girl Terence met earlier that week.

She immediately spots Terence, makes a quick surprised and disgusted face, and hurries

along with her family toward their table in t
he back.

"Ugh," Terence says, letting his head drop
onto the red plaid tablecloth with a thud. "Don't
look, you guys."

"Oh my," Claude's mom says.

"You know Novia?" Eddie says, leaning close
to Terence's face on the table.

Terence lifts his head and nods. "She's the
guitarist I auditioned the other night," he says.
"I told her she wasn't right for the band . . . but
I think she could tell I really meant she wasn't
good enough."

"Novia Pagano plays guitar too?" Claude
says, squinting at Terence in confusion.

James steps up to the table and smiles at
Claude's mom. "Are you folks ready to order?"
he asks, all smiles.

While Claude's mom places the order,
Terence leans across the table a little and says
quietly to Claude, "What do you mean, 'too'?"

Claude's mom finishes the order — a large pizza, half plain, half pineapple and ham, and a pitcher of pop — and then interrupts before Claude can reply. "Novia Pagano plays harp for the Catholic church."

"Harp?" Terence says.

"Sure, everyone knows that," Eddie says. "She's been taking lessons forever. Seriously, since, like, the day she was born."

"Oh," Terence says. "That lady was her harp teacher, not guitar teacher."

Eddie nods. "She's had a special solo in the holiday concert at the middle school for the last three years too. Didn't you see it in December?"

"Um, wasn't here yet," Terence says, "remember?"

"Oh, right," Eddie says. She shoves him gently, but Terence flops against the side of the booth. "I keep forgetting you're the new kid."

Terence rolls his eyes. "So she's really good?"

Claude nods. "Amazing."

His mom nods too.

Terence looks across the restaurant.
He can see the back of Melody's head from where he's sitting — her long black hair hanging over her shoulders and halfway down her back.

When she turns her head and looks back at him, he quickly looks away.

"You know," Claude says, "it might sound pretty cool to have a harp in the group."

Terence has been thinking the exact same thing.

"Totally," Eddie says. She waves over at Novia.

"Don't!" Terence says, grabbing her hand to stop her. "Even if she wanted to play harp with our band, she hates me now. And who could blame her?"

"Not me," Eddie says.

"Me either," Claude agrees.

"Anyway, so what?" Eddie says. "Let her hate you. We're not friends, right?"

"Right," Terence says.

"Cool," Eddie says as James steps up to the table with the pitcher of pop and four cups. "I'll have to brush up on my Joanna Newsom lyrics."

"Just don't kill your dinner with karate while you're here," he says. "I'm not cleaning up after you."

"Joanna Newsom jokes," Terence says as Claude's mom pours drinks. "Kind of impressive."

"Yeah, it's my daydream to impress a bunch of kids with my encyclopedic musical knowledge," James says as he walks off.

"That guy," Eddie says staring daggers into his back. "Anyway, better go and ask Novia if she wants to play harp for us."

"What, me?" Terence says. "No way."

"Why not?" Eddie says.

"Well, you know her better," Terence says. He looks at Claude. "You probably do too."

Claude takes a long drink of soda and then wipes his mouth with the back of his hand. "She goes to my church."

"Claude, use a napkin," his mom says, shoving one into his hand.

"Sorry, Mom."

Terence watches the exchange between mother and son, and he wants to smile and laugh and cry all at the same time.

He shakes his head. "I can't do it. She hates me."

"Maybe if you apologize and invite her to join us, she won't hate you anymore," Eddie suggests.

"Oh, right," Terence says. "'Oh, hi, Novia. You remember me? Sorry I said you suck at guitar. Wanna play harp for us?' That'll go really well."

"Fine," Eddie says, sliding out of the booth. "I'll do it. Baby."

Terence shrugs and watches Eddie weave between tables to the Paganos' booth. She talks to Novia for a moment.

Of course Terence can't make out a word of it, and he can't read lips.

But after a few words, both of them look back at Terence, and his face goes hot as he looks away.

When Eddie comes back, she slides in next to Terence — knocking into him a little too hard and obviously on purpose.

"She'll do it," she says.

"She will?" Terence says, genuinely surprised.

"Hates you, though," Eddie says. "You were right about that."

She's not as mean to Terence as he fears though when she joins them in Claude's basement the next morning.

Not that he cares one way or the other, of course. He's not looking for friends. But he is looking for a great band.

And that he's got.

Novia's harp playing is lovely. At times he almost feels redundant himself, since her fingers move over the strings of her harp, striking bass notes as often as treble.

They can work on that, and it'll be worth it. Her ear for modes and scales and improvising are flawless.

"So," Novia says after the song ends. She lowers her harp and looks squarely at Terence, "How'd I do?"

"Great," Terence says, forcing himself to look back at her. "That was fantastic."

"Thank you," Novia says, crossing her arms and leaning back a bit on her stool. "Now do you guys have a drummer, or . . . ?"

Terence, Eddie, and Claude exchange quick glances.

"Um, no," Terence says. "Why, do you think we need one?"

Novia shrugs and makes a bored *none of my business* face.

"My old band had a drummer," Terence says. "I'm not *against* it or anything." He looks at Eddie.

"I'm not against it either," she says. "But I don't know anyone."

"Yeah, you do," Claude says. "Henry Park is in jazz band with your brother."

"Oh, but he—" Eddie starts. She stops herself.

"He what?" Terence says.

"He's terrible," Claude says as his fingers move mindlessly and quietly over the keyboard.

"Like, he's a bad person?" Terence asks.

"Oh, no!" Eddie says quickly. "He's really nice."

"*Really* nice," Novia says.

"He's fine." Claude shrugs. "But he can't play."

"But he's in Bonk's jazz band?" Terence says, somewhat confused.

The others nod.

"I don't understand," Terence finally admits. "What do you mean?"

"And finally the Hart Arts boy gets a glimpse of the seedy and untalented underbelly of public middle school music programs," Eddie says.

"So anyone who wants to join can just join?" Terence asks.

The others nod again.

"Huh," Terence says. "That's kinda nice, actually. It's not like they're playing halls or going on tour."

"Maybe we should try the high school," Claude says.

"Are you kidding me?" Eddie says. "No way. Not happening."

Novia shakes her head. "No way. My brother is in high school. A senior. And no way. I don't want some greasy, smelly eighteen-year-old with a beard, and who probably smokes, hanging around the band."

Eddie points at Novia. "Mmhm. No way."

"Come on," Claude says, turning on his bench to argue with the girls. "We have no other option."

"What if we put an age limit," Terence says, "like sixteen?"

Eddie and Novia look at each other and seem to speak silently. Then they both nod. "Fine."

"If I make some flyers, can you ask your brother to hang them around the high school?" Terence says.

Novia bites her lip. "I guess," she says. "But that doesn't mean he'll do it."

"Good enough," Terence says. "I'll think of some other places to put them too."

LOCAL BAND
looking for
DRUMMER/ PERCUSSION
for
JAZZ/ROCK/ SOUL/R&B

Must be very good and 16 or younger.
Must have your own kit.

Text Terence 952-555-0514

CHAPTER FIVE

First thing Monday morning, Terence grabs his phone to check for texts. Nothing — aside from one from Eddie: *Any texts yet???*

"Morning," Dad says when Terence drags himself into the kitchen. He's dressed in tan pants and a clean green sweater, and sitting at the table flipping through one of those thick magazines that just shows up at the house and no one ever ordered. A full cup of coffee sits steaming in the middle of the table.

"Sleep OK?" Dad asks.

"Um, yeah. Fine," Terence says. "What are you doing up so early?"

"Can't a guy make breakfast for his son before school?" He puts the magazine down on the table.

"Theoretically, I guess," Terence says.

"What'll you have?"

"I'm not that hungry," Terence says.

'Oh, come on," Dad says, smiling as he gets up and goes to the fridge. "It's the most important meal of the day."

"A bagel, I guess," Terence says. "Half a bagel. With cream cheese."

"There we go," Dad says, opening the freezer and pulling out the plastic bag of bagels. "Coming right up."

They're both quiet for a minute while Dad pulls apart a frozen bagel, puts half in the toaster, and pushes it down.

"Dad," Terence says.

"Hm?" his dad grunts.

Then his dad gets the cream cheese tub and a knife.

"What's going on with you?" Terence asks.

"What do you mean?" Dad says without looking at him.

"For months you've been . . ."

"Depressed?"

"Yeah," Terence says. "I mean, I get that. But the last couple of days, you've been getting dressed, going out. I don't even know where you go some afternoons."

"Wait a second," Dad says, smirking. "Who's the dad here? You have to know where I am all the time?"

"That's not what I mean."

"I know," Dad says.

The bagel pops up, and he quickly smears some cream cheese across its face. Then drops the plate in front of Terence's spot at the table and sits across from him.

Dad takes a deep breath and sighs. "I've been seeing a psychiatrist."

Terence stares down at the bagel. "Like, a therapist?"

Dad nods. "That's the general idea," he says. "I know I've been a mess since Mom passed, and it's not fair to you. It's not even fair to *me*."

Terence shrugs. He doesn't want Dad to think *his* sadness is hurting Terence somehow — though it is.

"So I decided to do something about it," Dad goes on. He runs a finger around the rim of his untouched coffee cup. "I've been to see Dr. Hyacinth four times so far. I think she's really helping."

"Good," Terence says, because what else can he say? It makes no sense that Dad acting a little happier and more normal has Terence feeling somehow even sadder than before.

Dad pushes his chair back and stands up. "Eat

up," he says. "I'll give you a lift to school if you want. Got some errands to do this morning."

"OK." Terence takes a bite of his bagel, but when Dad's out of the room, he dumps it in the trash and goes to brush his teeth.

"Nothing," Terence says when he finds Claude, Eddie, and Novia waiting for him near the front doors after school as the buses are loading.

"Not even one text?" Claude says. "I don't get it."

"I do," Novia says. "My brother is a jerk."

"That's true," Eddie says, "but what does that have to do with anything?"

"He probably spread the word at the high school that no one should answer the flyer," Novia says.

"Seriously?" Terence says, irritated.

"I wouldn't put it past him," Novia says.

"Gotta catch my bus. Don't want to miss my lesson today."

"We should go too," Eddie says, grabbing Terence's arm.

"And I have hockey practice," Claude says. "But don't worry. Someone will want to join. Meanwhile, we can keep having rehearsals as a quartet."

"True," Terence concedes, and he lets Eddie pull him to the bus.

When he gets home, Dad's out. "Probably at the doctor again," he mutters to himself.

But the fridge is restocked, and the dishes are clean, and the laundry is done. Maybe Dad's doing the right thing getting some help.

Still, Terence can't help feeling a little resentful that Dad might just be *done* mourning. Terence will never be done.

He pulls the tub of peanut butter from the fridge and opens a new pack of Oreos. The first cookie breaks when he uses it to scoop up some peanut butter. "Dang."

His phone vibrates on the table, making him jump. He grabs the phone, hopeful that a drummer has finally replied to their ad.

But nope. Just Eddie: *Anything?*

Terence rolls his eyes. He was sitting next to her on the bus literally ten minutes ago. He's about to type back a reply when the phone shakes again.

"Jeez, Eddie," he mumbles as he pulls down the notification, but it's not from her. It's from a number he doesn't recognize.

Saw your flyer. I'd like to audition. -J

Terence quickly forwards the text to the others, adding: *Anyone know who this is?*

No!

Nope.

DID YOU WRITE BACK?!

The last one's from Eddie, of course.

Terence stares at the text from J, thinking. Finally he types back, *We can come to you. Where's your kit?*

The reply comes right away: *I can travel. Have a car too. Say when and where.*

Terence sends a reply to his bandmates. *Tomorrow afternoon OK with everyone?*

Yes!

5? Can't miss hockey.

YES

So Terence replies with Claude's address, and J says it's fine: *See you then.*

"I told him 5:15," Terence says when the four bandmates are gathered in Claude's basement the next afternoon. "So we have time to talk first."

"About what?" Eddie says, sneering.

"What if he's terrible?" Terence says. "What are we looking for, anyway? Do we have a style in mind?"

"Versatility," Claude says. "If he's sixteen, he probably only plays heavy. Can he dial it back for jazz?"

"He saw the flyer," Novia points out. "If he didn't like jazz, he wouldn't be coming down here."

"He might if he's desperate to join a band," Terence points out. "I mean, I would."

Claude's mom calls down the basement steps. "Aren't you guys expecting a drummer?"

"Yeah, Mom!" Claude calls back. "Is he here?"

"Must be," she replies. "But he doesn't have drums."

Terence stands. "They're probably still in his car," he says. "Let's go help him unload."

But when he and Eddie are halfway up the steps, the drummer appears at the top and says, "Nothing to unload — Oh."

"Oh," Terence echoes.

"Oh," Eddie repeats.

Because the boy standing in the doorway at the top of the steps is none other than James, the rudest server at Paulie's Pizza.

CHAPTER SIX

"So," James says, sitting on the old basement couch. No one has said anything since Claude's mom excused herself and James sat down. They've just sat there, staring at their hands, looking at James, a little confused. "I didn't know it was you three — er, four."

"Hi," Novia says.

"Hi," James says.

"You don't have any drums," Terence says.

James pats the black hardcase on the couch beside him. It looks a bit like the sort of briefcase you always see in movies and TV shows when someone has to make a huge illicit payment in cash, except it's not handcuffed to his wrist and James is wearing skinny jeans, a hoodie, and a parka with a fur-trimmed hood instead of a black suit and dark glasses.

"Everything I need is in here," he says, "if I can plug into your PA?"

"So, what?" Eddie says. She's standing in the middle of the room, sneering down at him. "You're like Skrillex or something?"

"Not exactly," James says. "But I can program or improvise a drum track to whatever you four can play. I guarantee that."

He pulls off his parka, turns sideways on the couch, and pops open the briefcase. "Play something," he says. "And give me a few minutes to program. You'll see."

Terence shrugs and picks up his bass. Claude warms up with a few arpeggios, and Novia makes the harp sing. Eddie flips on the PA.

"Um, 'Now At Last'?" Terence says.

"Blossom Dearie," Eddie says. "Got it."

Claude plays the intro. Terence joins in. Novia listens for the changes and lays down a rich harp part. When Eddie starts singing, the whole package is lovely.

James sits focused on his open laptop as he pulls on headphones and uncovers one ear to listen to the band. After the first refrain, he unwinds a cable, crosses to the PA system at Eddie's feet, and plugs in. Then he returns to his laptop and clicks the mouse.

The speakers click and hiss as James's beat joins the band. Instantly, what had been a classic bebop sound zooms into the 21st century with the sparse electronic drum sounds, as if cool jazz and dance music had a baby.

Terence watches James click around on his laptop, his head nodding to his own beat.

He wants to hate it. He wants to tell James to get out and take his computer with him and to never darken their doorway again. He wants to say, *And we won't be eating at Paulie's anymore, either!*

But he can't. Because it sounds amazing. And looking around at his bandmates' faces, he sees they feel the same way. Eddie looks irritated and delighted at the same time — maybe irritated that she's delighted.

When the song's over, even James looks pleasantly surprised. "Wow," he says.

"Yeah," Novia says.

"That was really, really cool," Eddie admits, dropping onto the old recliner in the corner. It creaks as she leans back and kicks out her feet.

"I gotta admit," James says. "I didn't think you guys would sound very good. But you do. You're a talented bunch of kids."

"Hey," Novia says. "We're not *kids* any more than you are."

"I don't know," James says. "I have a job. And a car."

Novia frowns at him.

"Look, the point is," James says, "your sound is pretty classic and you all have skills. I think I can add something fresh, though."

"Yeah, I agree," Terence says. "So you'll join?"

James looks at him like he's crazy. "Are you kidding?" he says. "Obviously."

Terence smiles and sighs. "All right," he says. "I think this band is finally complete."

Claude plays a celebratory run up the piano. "Now we just need a name."

"Oh, I've got that covered," James says. "The James Gang. I've been saving it."

"Excuse me?" Eddie says, putting a fist on a hip.

"You've been saving it," Terence says, laughing, "but you never googled it. There already was a James Gang."

"What?" James says. "Really?"

Terence nods. "Listen to the classic rock

station once in a while," he says. "Anyway, we're not naming the band after you."

Eddie opens her mouth to say something, but Terence keeps going, cutting her off.

"Not after me, either," he says. "Don't worry."

"Let's do a few more," Claude says, and then adds, leaning around the piano to see James on the couch, "unless you have to get to your job in your car?"

"Ha." James laughs. "I got the night off. I can play as late as you guys can, unless you're bedtimes are really early?"

Eddie throws a little pillow across the room and it hits James in the face.

Novia plucks her harp — the opening of Joanna Newsom's "The Book of Right On."

"Ah!" Eddie says, leaping up from her chair. "I knew it. I can totally sing this."

"It's pretty high," Novia says over her own staccato playing.

"I'll bring it down an octave," Eddie says. "It'll sound good."

And she starts, and it does sound good — rich and a little creepy. James obviously knows the song, because he joins in with his electronic beats right away. It's not the frenetic hip-hop beat the Roots used when they sampled the same song. It's half the speed, sparse and laid back.

Terence follows the musical cues, and his bass line is barely there. When Claude joins in, his piano part contributes some hushed background tones. Add it all up, and the sound was beyond anything Terence thought this band could be.

The new band plays till after eight, when Claude's mom finally makes them stop and reminds them all they have homework they should probably being doing. Even James's eyes go wide at that.

They break for the night and go their

separate ways. Eddie's mom gives Terence a ride home again, this time without the difficult, heavy condolences.

But when Terence unlocks the door to the rental house and steps inside, he finds Dad.

And it's not the new dad — the one in khakis and a sweater and a smile. This is the dad he's known for the last six months, on his back on the couch, the TV on and his eyes closed.

Terence pulls the blanket from the back of the couch and lays it over his father and kisses his cheek.

"Night, Dad," Terence says. "See you in the morning."

CHAPTER SEVEN

"Did you get the email from James?" Eddie says as she slides into the empty spot next to Terence on the bus on Monday morning.

Terence nods. "Sounds really good."

James — the new "drummer" and their waiter at Paulie's — managed to get a recording of two songs at his audition and their first practice together the night before. He set up a couple of microphones and connected his laptop to the PA output.

"We have a demo, Terence," Eddie says,

leaning back in her seat like she just finished a great meal.

"They sound good," Terence says. "But we should get them sounding perfect before we play it for people."

"I already played it for Luke," she says. "And my mom and dad."

"Well, that's fine," Terence says.

"And everyone at the bus stop," Eddie says.

"Oh."

"And I put it on my YouTube channel."

"What?!" Terence says, sitting bolt upright.

"Kidding," Eddie says. "Relax. I don't have a YouTube channel."

"Whew," Terence says, and then adds, "We should probably start one."

Eddies laughs as the bus pulls up to the curb in front of Franklin Middle and squeaks to a stop.

It's a good day at school. Terence sees Novia

in advisory, and they secretly listen to the demo together, sharing earbuds in the back of the classroom.

He sees Claude in the halls and they give each other a thumbs-up. "Demo sounds sick, T!" Claude says.

He eats lunch with Eddie and her brother. Even Luke admits the songs sound good.

When he climbs on the bus at the end of the day, Eddie has a seat saved for him. His phone shakes in his pocket. It's a group text from James to the band: *Can't stop listening to our songs!*

When he walks from the bus stop to his house along Maybe It's Not So Bad Living Here After All Lane, he's feeling pretty good. But when he opens the door, there's Dad, lying on the couch in his pajama pants and a ragged T-shirt.

"You awake?" Terence says as he drops his book bag next to the couch in the small living room.

The TV is on, and Dad's eyes are open but glazed. He's staring at the TV, but he doesn't seem to really see it.

"Dad?" Terence sits on the arm of the couch near Dad's feet.

"Hi, kid," Dad says in a distant voice. He's as far away as ever, as if the last couple of weeks of relative happiness never happened.

Maybe he's even worse.

"Did you see Dr. Hyacinth today?" Terence says.

Dad pulls his red and wet eyes from the TV to look at Terence. "No," he says. "I'm not going to see her anymore."

"Why not?"

Dad forces himself to sit up. "I'm pretty depressed, Terence."

"Of course you are," Terence says. "So am I."

"You're doing well, though," Dad says. He sounds like he might cry.

Terence's phone shakes in his pocket.

"See that?" Dad says. "You just got a text. Probably from that girl with a boy's name."

"Eddie," Terence confirms.

Dad shakes his head and lets his head fall back to look at the ceiling. "You've got friends. You're doing so well at your new school. And I still feel terrible, every day about everything."

"I do too," Terence says. He's not sure it's true, but it's sometimes true.

Dad pulls Terence by the arm till he's sitting next to him. "I wanted Dr. Hyacinth to fix me," Dad says. "I thought it'd be like getting antibiotics for an infection. Like, she'd give me a pill, and I'd feel all better. I wouldn't be sad anymore."

"People take pills for depression."

"That's not how Dr. Hyacinth sees it," Dad says. "She says I'm not depressed. She says I'm mourning, and that's not a clinical condition. She recommended talk therapy, not medication."

"Makes sense," Terence says.

"I know," Dad says nodding. "It just sounds a whole lot harder."

The TV is playing an old *X-Files* episode. Terence and Dad sit together and watch till the commercial break.

Terence pulls out his phone. The text is from Eddie, but he doesn't read it. Instead he opens his music player.

"Listen to this, Dad," he says, and he taps play on their version of "Now At Last."

It opens with just Claude's piano and Eddie's vocals.

Dad smiles a tiny bit as he stares down at the phone in Terence's hand: just that blank CD art and the little blue bar at the bottom crawling from left to right.

The harps come in with Terence's bass, followed closely by James's slow and sparse beat, and Dad actually flinches in surprise.

"This is really nice," he says. "It's not Billie

Holiday, obviously. A remix of her, maybe?"

Terence smiles and shakes his head.

"No, she never sang this, I bet, " Dad says. "Did you make this?"

"Sort of," Terence says as Novia takes a short harp solo after the second refrain. "That's me on bass."

Dad's eyes go wide, and he flashes his proud smile. Terence hasn't seen it in a while.

"No kidding?" Dad says. "You know this is one of my favorite songs. Mom loved it."

"I know."

"Makes it kind of bittersweet right now," Dad admits. "So who's singing?"

"That's Eddie," Terence says.

"What?" Dad says, stunned. "So this is your new band?"

Terence nods.

"Don't play it for Polly," Dad says. "This girl's better."

"Dad," Terence says, shaking his head.

They listen to the rest of the track and the next one, Dad with an arm around Terence's shoulders the whole time, hardly speaking except to say things like, "Amazing," and "Ooh, that was nice."

When the songs are done, Dad gives Terence an extra squeeze, turns off the TV, and stands up. "Mac and cheese tonight?" he says.

They go to the kitchen together to make supper.

MUSIC TRIVIA

Think you have what it takes to join Terence Kato's band? Take this music trivia quiz and find out!

1. What is the level and intensity of sound measured in?
   A. Decibels
   B. Gigabytes
   C. Vibrato

2. A musical scale comprises how many notes?
   A. 16
   B. 8
   C. 10

3. What term describes people singing without instruments?
   A. Solo
   B. Allegro
   C. A cappella

4. What term describes the section of a song that is repeated after each verse?
   A. Beat
   B. Chorus
   C. Choir

5. What term describes how high or low a musical sound is?
   A. Pitch
   B. Range
   C. Volume

6. What is the highest singing voice called?
   A. Baritone
   B. Tenor
   C. Soprano

7. How many musical instruments make up a quartet?
   A. 4
   B. 14
   C. 8

8. What Italian word means "growing louder?"
   A. Crescendo
   B. Bass
   C. Allegro

9. What are all instruments that are played by being hit with something called?
   A. Brass
   B. Woodwinds
   C. Percussion

10. What is the lowest singing voice called?
    A. Baritone
    B. Tenor
    C. Soprano

Answers: 1. A 2. B 3. C 4. B 5. A 6. C
7. A 8. A 9. C 10. A

BOY
SEEKING
BAND

STEVE BREZENOFF

Steve Brezenoff is the author of more than fifty middle-grade chapter books, including the Field Trip Mysteries series, the Ravens Pass series of thrillers, and the Return to the Titanic series. He's also written three young-adult novels, *Guy in Real Life*; *Brooklyn, Burning*; and *The Absolute Value of -1*. In his spare time, he enjoys video games, cycling, and cooking. Steve lives in Minneapolis with his wife, Beth, and their son and daughter.